No Two Snowflakes

written by *Sheree Fitch*
illustrated by *Janet Wilson*

ORCA BOOK PUBLISHERS

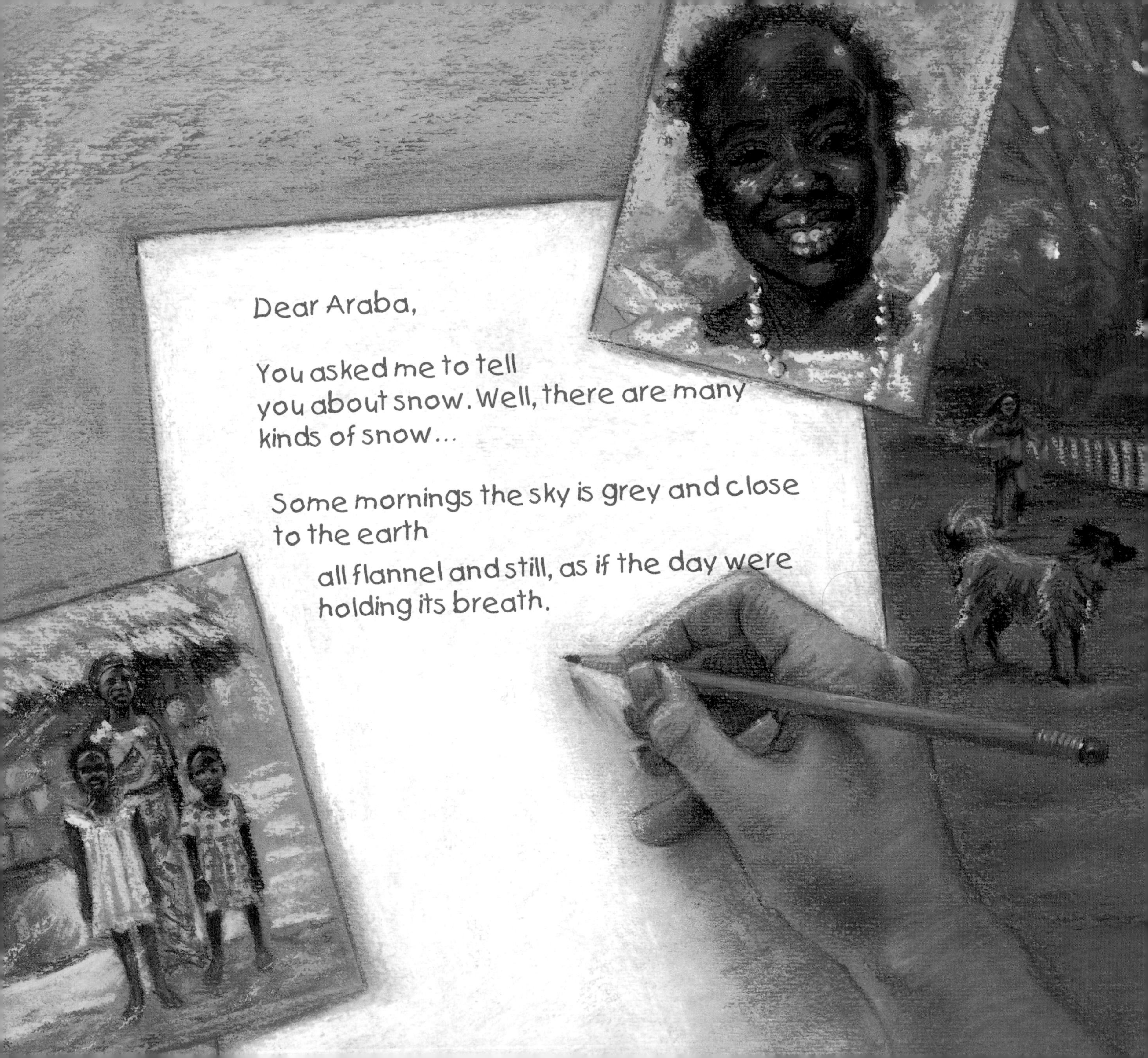

Dear Araba,

You asked me to tell
you about snow. Well, there are many
kinds of snow...

Some mornings the sky is grey and close
to the earth

all flannel and still, as if the day were
holding its breath.

Then, with no one noticing when it begins, snow

f
a
l
l
s

in slow feathershapes
settles on cheeks
kisses eyelids.

Hold out your tongue, for the taste of snow is white.

Some days, snow is splinter sharp
needlepoints in skin
sounds like small stones
thrown at windows.

Turn your back to the wind, come in
by the fire with me.
We'll sip hot chocolate, eat cinnamon toast
tell stories till we nod asleep
to the snapcrackle music of wood
burning
the sifting sound
of snow drifting
against glass.

On a bluesky day when the air is peppermint clean
we find a hill, waddle up a long slope
dragging toboggans behind.
This snow speaks too
squeaks a rubbery language beneath our feet
snow's laughter
the sound of balloons scritching together.

Let's
ride
down
let's
slide
down
wind scratching our cheeks
snow spraying our faces
praying our ride will last all the way
into
tomorrow.

Frozen on the ground, snow
crisp as crust shines back at the moon
such polished fields and hills of wax

a lip-chattery world
of step-slippery snow.

Listen to its cccrrunnchchch.
See how far we can walk
before snowcrust breaks
before we sink through to fluffy stuff below.

Let's make-believe we've landed
on the surface of the moon.
Astronauts, we explore an unknown
lunar landscape.

The snow that sticks in small white pebbles
to woolen mittens
is snowball snow
    snowman snow
        packing snow
for snow forts, igloos, tunnels.

Let's make a secret underworld
and play there all the afternoon
until indigo shadows dance across the yard
telling time for supper.

Then there is snow that refuses to go when the world
turns warm again   stubborn
humps of mud-splattered snow
hiding from the heat
until the fingers of the sun find it   finally
scrub the last of it
a   w   a   y.

Snow   sometimes sugar frosting

Snow   sometimes windwhipped waves of white

Snow sometimes designs you find in dunes of sand

Snow sometimes the trace of bird feet or a secret code left by rabbit paws.

The trees after snow?

Branches wearing long white gloves

crystal chandeliers in a palace of glass

stillness

emptiness

That's all I know, Araba ...
I have tried to tell you the taste and smell of snow
its sound and touch

but words are not enough.

To know snow
you must hold it in your hands
feel it melt to pearls of water
until it is gone ...

But wait ... one more thing ...
Sometimes snow can be ... angel feathers!

Here's what we can do ...

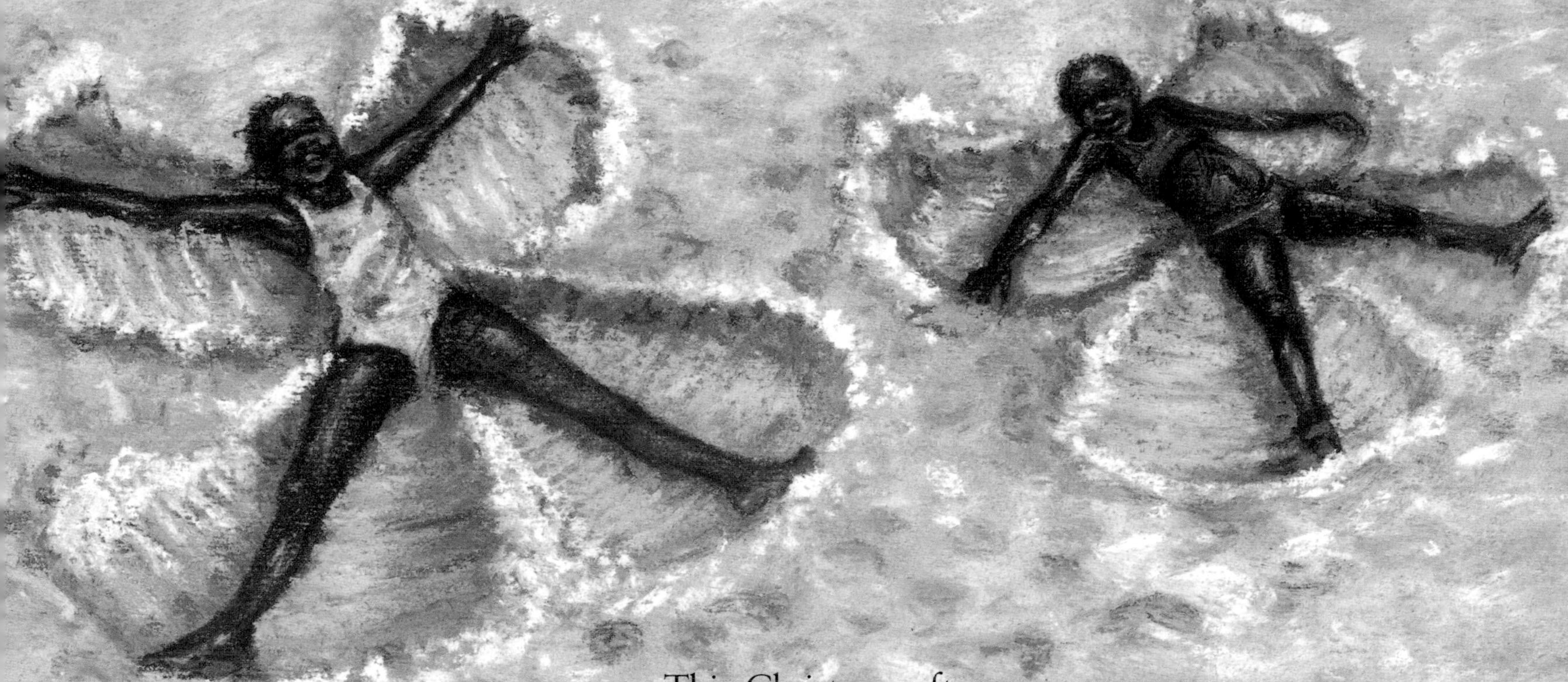

This Christmas afternoon
I will take my brother out in our backyard.
We will lie on our backs
swing our arms and legs in wide arcs
make angels in the snow
while you take your sister
to the shore of the sea
and, just for us, make angels in the sand.

Snow is not sand, sand is not snow   but ...

on this day of miracles
remember that the sun you see
is the sun we see
that no two snowflakes are alike

No two snowflakes are alike

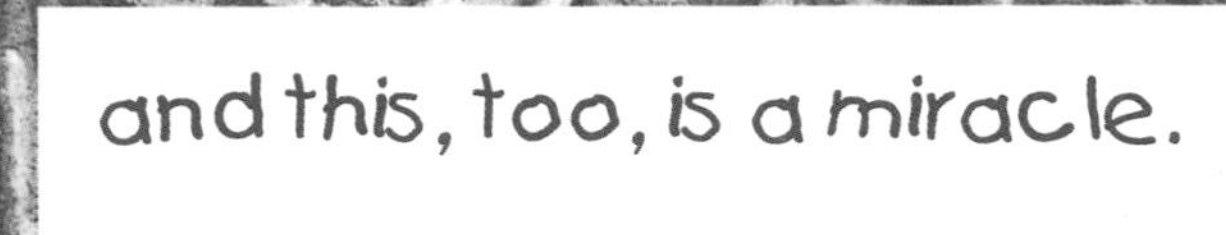
and this, too, is a miracle.
Love, Lou

Dear Reader:

I was in grade two when I first heard the words "No two snowflakes are alike."

"But," I said to my teacher, Mrs. Goodwin, "how do we know this for sure? Has anyone ever seen all the snowflakes that have ever fallen? Does anybody know this for sure?"

She smiled and repeated, "No two snowflakes are alike – just like no two people are alike."

I still wasn't sure I got it. Our class made paper snowflakes and pasted pictures of our faces in the center of each snowflake. When we came in the next morning, they were twirling from the ceiling of our classroom. Wow. Our "differences" were beautiful.

In that same class I was studying geography. My heart thump bumped in my chest whenever Mrs. Goodwin pulled down the map and got out her pointer. The world. The whole world! We learned about China. We learned words like "rickshaw" and "sampans." We learned about the continent of Africa, words like "savannah" and the customs of peoples a world away from my Canadian home. Sometimes I would look up at the sun and wonder if children in a far-off place were looking up at that same sun thinking of me thinking of them. Or the same moon at night, or the same stars.

To me, that idea was a kind of magic. That was the year I knew I wanted to grow up to be a writer. It was the year I began to dream of visiting another culture.

Many years later, as part of an exchange program run by Rick McDaniel, the International Director at Fredericton's YMCA, I visited the country of Belize in Central America. I went into schools, read my poetry and shared stories with children and their teachers. It was my first trip ever outside of Canada.

One day a boy said to me, "Miss Sheree, tell me about that snow in Canada." I tried to tell him. I really tried. But I could not imagine how it would be never ever to have felt or tasted snow. Only when I was home again was I able to begin the answer that has become this poem and this book.

Every book, like every person and every snowflake, is different too. I am honored once again to be bringing out a book for UNICEF to use in its ongoing work. UNICEF celebrates differences, encouraging us to look beyond the borders of our own experiences. In UNICEF programs around the world, dedicated educators like my own Mrs. Goodwin make magical links for their students through creative teaching activities. Dinny Biggs, a teacher-volunteer with UNICEF Canada, has created inspiring activities and ideas related to this book for teachers, parents and children to use if they choose. Several of these activities are listed below.

Even now I marvel at the miracle of each snowflake being different. Sometimes I look up at the sky and wonder if someone is thinking of me thinking of them thinking of me thinking of them. And guess what? I still make snow angels in winter and sand angels in summer.

Hope you do too!

Yours truly,

Sheree Fitch

Celebrate your senses.

a) Collect objects that are referred to in the poem by their scent: cinnamon, peppermint and wood, for example. Blindfold friends or parents and see if they can identify the objects by smell alone. No touching!

b) Find things that are referred to in the poem by their feel, such as ice chips, a wet wool mitten and a container of snow. Place them one at a time in a bag and see if your friends can tell what they are by touching them. They have to be brave enough to put their hands inside that bag!

c) Create a soundscape by tape-recording the sounds referred to in the poem, by recording things that sound like them. How could you imitate the sound of a fire crackling, for example, or the sound of booted feet walking in dry snow? See if your friends can guess what the sounds are supposed to be and how you made them.

When you are done, celebrate your sense of taste with mugs of hot chocolate and triangles of cinnamon toast.

For more ideas, visit the UNICEF website at www.unicef.ca/eng/unicef/notwosnowflakes.

Library and Archives Canada Cataloguing in Publication

Fitch, Sheree.
No two snowflakes

ISBN 10: 1-55143-227-7 / ISBN 13: 978-1-55143-227-4

1. Snow—Juvenile fiction. I. Wilson, Janet, 1952- II. Title.
PS8561.I86N62 2001 jC813'.54 C2001-910579-7
PZ7.F5615No 2001

First published in the United States, 2002
Library of Congress Control Number: 2001089946

Orca Book Publishers gratefully acknowledges the support for its publishing programs provided by the following agencies: the Government of Canada through the Book Publishing Industry Development Program and the Canada Council for the Arts, and the Province of British Columbia through the BC Arts Council and the Book Publishing Tax Credit.

Design and typesetting by Christine Toller

Orca Book Publishers
PO Box 5626, Stn. B
Victoria, BC Canada
V8R 6S4

Orca Book Publishers
PO Box 468
Custer, WA USA
98240-0468

www.orcabook.com
Printed and bound in China.
11 10 09 08 • 7 6 5 4